OCTONAUTS™

Search and Find

As the Octonaut's marine biologist, Shellington is always searching for sea life.

Can you help find the creatures on the following pages as we travel through the sunlight, twilight and midnight zones? Octonauts, let's do this!

SIMON AND SCHUSTER

SUNLIGHT ZONE: TIDE POOLS
Tide pools are small pools of trapped seawater.

These pools are formed when the tide goes out. When the tide comes back in, they are covered with water again. Tough sea creatures live here, because they have to live with constant changes in their environment.

CAN YOU FIND?

2 ANEMONES

HERMIT CRAB

SEA URCHIN

KWAZII

24 BARNACLES

6 SHELLS

9 STARFISH

5 CORAL

SUNLIGHT ZONE: KELP FOREST

In a kelp forest, each tall kelp plant protects many creatures. At the top, fish glide beneath the leaves, and at the bottom near the roots, crabs and urchins can easily hide. It's a bit hard for a gup to get through, though!

CAN YOU FIND?

SWELL SHARK

4 SEA SNAILS

2 CUTTLEFISH

7 SEA HORSES

OCTOPUS

8 KELPFISH

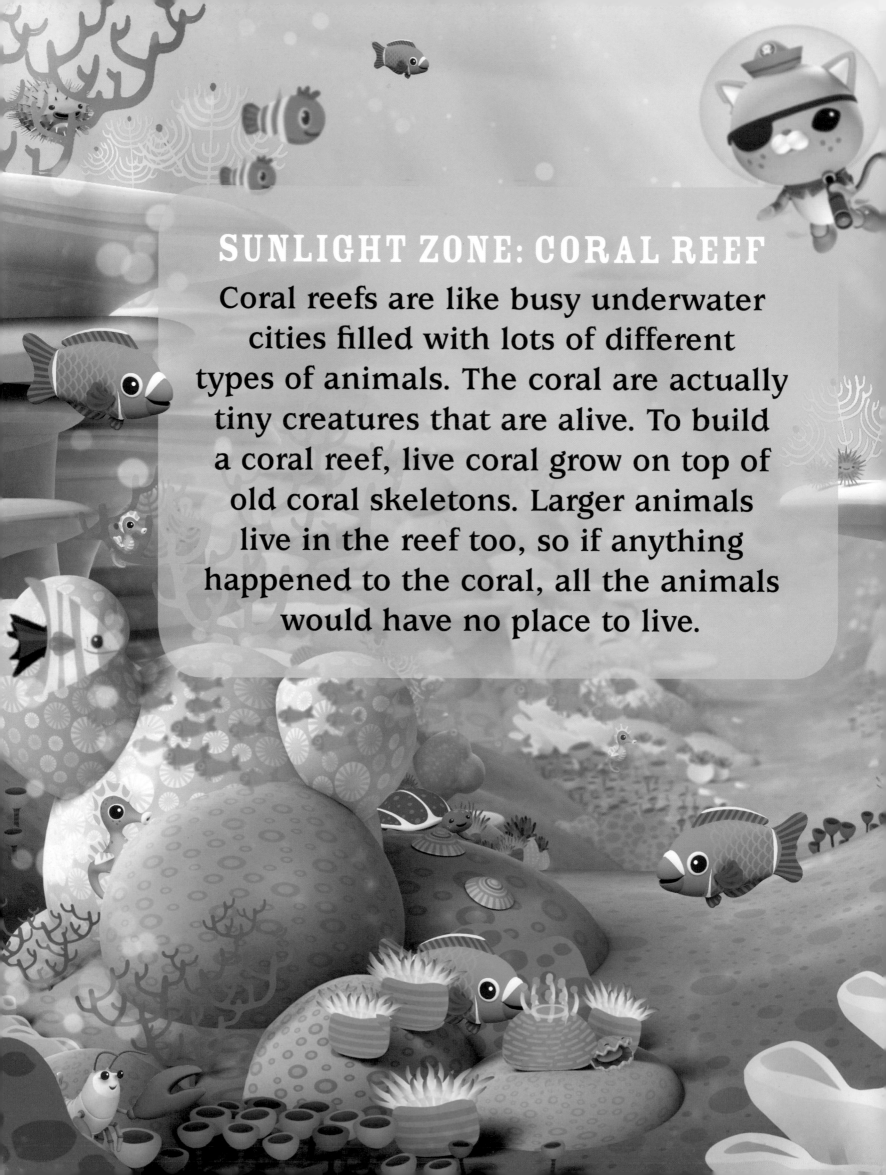

SUNLIGHT ZONE: CORAL REEF

Coral reefs are like busy underwater cities filled with lots of different types of animals. The coral are actually tiny creatures that are alive. To build a coral reef, live coral grow on top of old coral skeletons. Larger animals live in the reef too, so if anything happened to the coral, all the animals would have no place to live.

CAN YOU FIND?

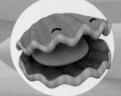
MORAY EEL

GIANT CLAM

SNAPPING SHRIMP

CUTTLEFISH

OCTOPUS

PUFFERFISH

LEATHERBACK SEA TURTLE

7 SEAHORSES

7 PARROT FISH

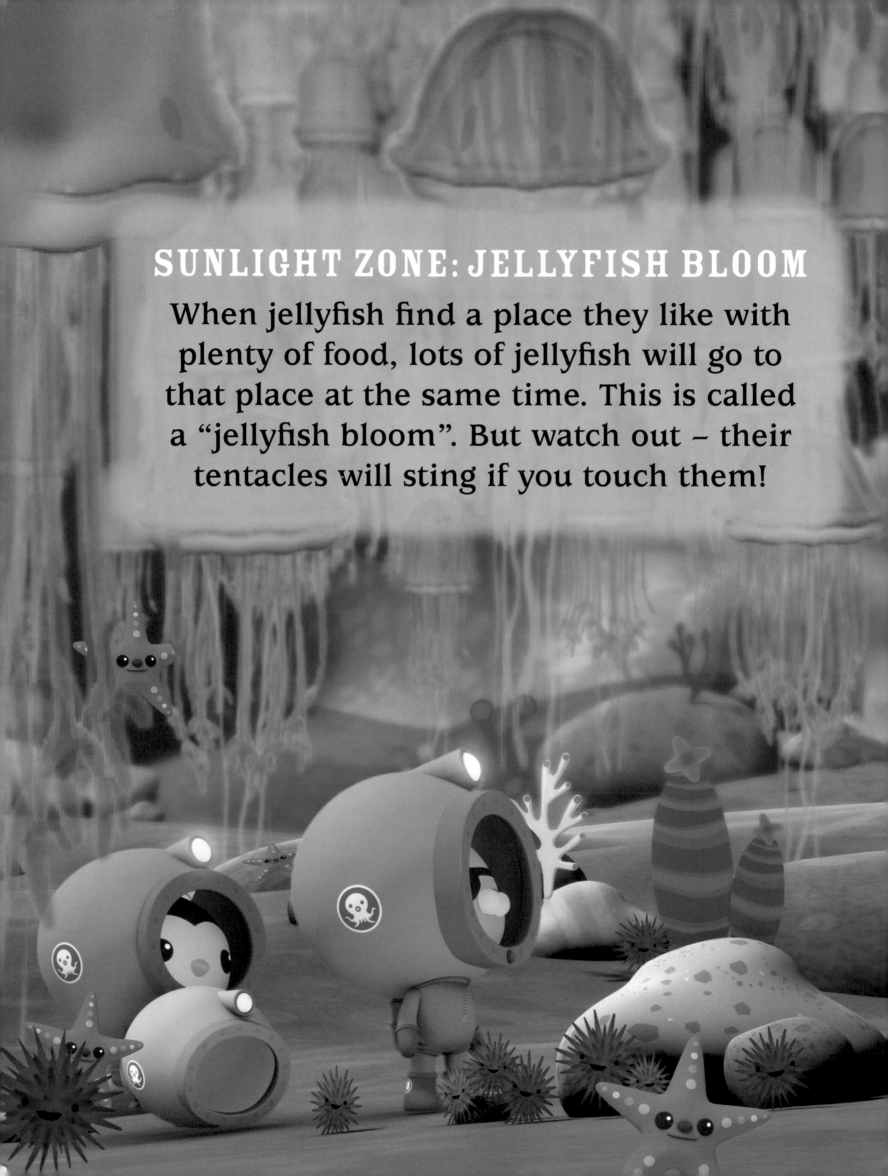

SUNLIGHT ZONE: JELLYFISH BLOOM

When jellyfish find a place they like with plenty of food, lots of jellyfish will go to that place at the same time. This is called a "jellyfish bloom". But watch out – their tentacles will sting if you touch them!

CAN YOU FIND?

13 SMILEY SEA URCHINS

4 OCTONAUTS SYMBOLS

7 STARFISH

SUNLIGHT ZONE: TROPICAL WATER

Humpback whales swim from cold, polar water where they eat to warm, tropical waters to mate. If humpback whales get too much sun, they can get sunburned! This albino humpback whale is very rare – he's all white, which means he's more likely to get sunburned.

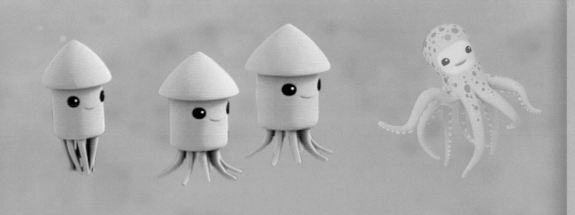

He needs some mushroom coral!
Mushroom coral live in tropical
waters too and make their own
oily, oozy suncream.

CAN YOU FIND?

BARNACLES

KWAZII

DASHI

PESO

TWEAK

SHELLINGTON

9 KELPFISH

4 OCTOPUSES

SUNLIGHT ZONE: SHIPWRECK

Shipwrecks may be the result of
dangerous pirate activity, but they also
provide shelter for small creatures.
Over time, these man-made objects
become artificial reefs, providing
hiding places for marine life.

CAN YOU FIND?

SPYGLASS

MAP

PIRATE FLAG

TREASURE

2 OCTONAUTS SYMBOLS

18 STARFISH

6 SEA SNAILS

TWILIGHT ZONE: SEAMOUNT

A seamount is an underwater mountain formed from volcanic activity. Many creatures like coral and fish live near seamounts because there's lots of food. The ocean current goes up the steep slopes of the seamount, carrying food upwards from the depths of the oceans.

CAN YOU FIND?

BLUE CRAB   **SNOT SEA CUCUMBER**

REEF LOBSTER   **ELECTRIC TORPEDO RAY**

OCTOPUS   **CUTTLEFISH**

BARNACLES

14 ANEMONES   **6 SEA SNAILS**

7 GREEN KELP FISH   **8 BRITTLE STARS**

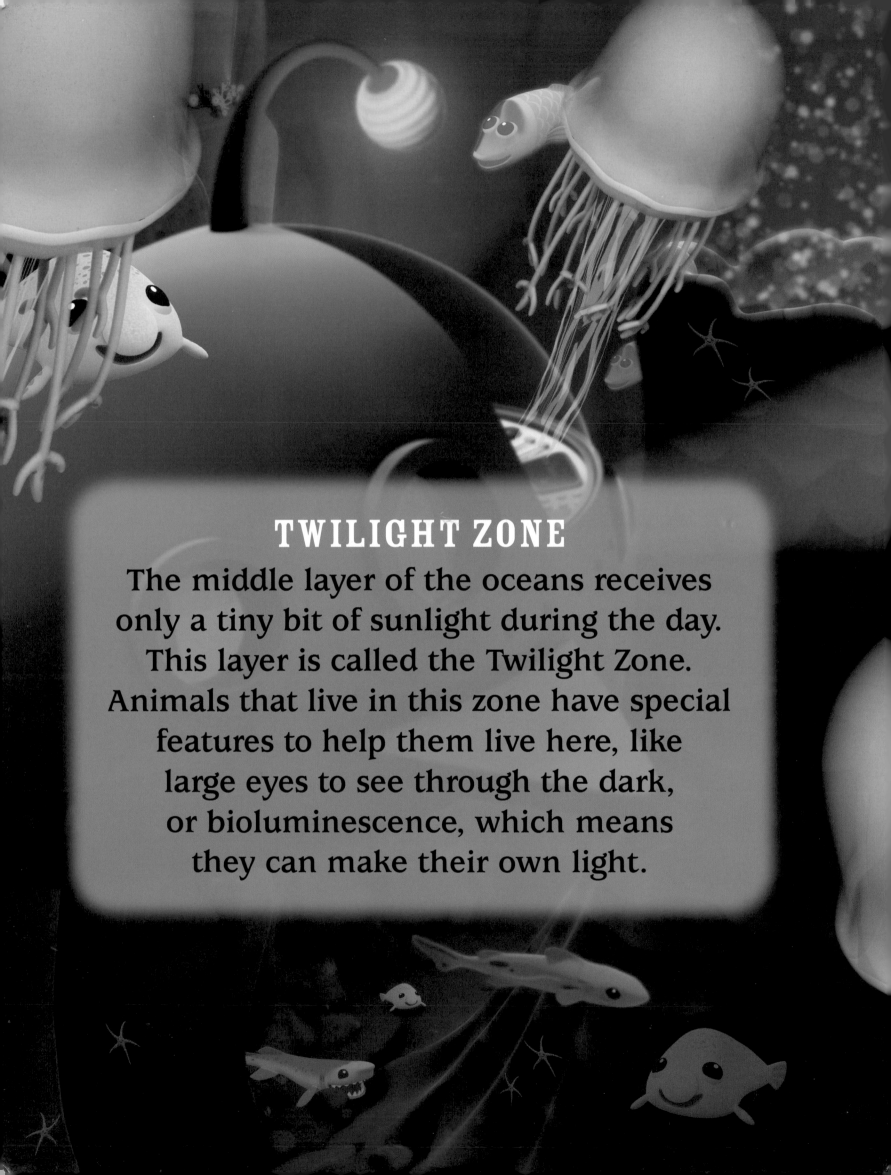

TWILIGHT ZONE

The middle layer of the oceans receives
only a tiny bit of sunlight during the day.
This layer is called the Twilight Zone.
Animals that live in this zone have special
features to help them live here, like
large eyes to see through the dark,
or bioluminescence, which means
they can make their own light.

5 BLOBFISH

8 BRITTLE SEA STAR

4 COOKIECUTTER SHARKS

5 SPOOKFISH

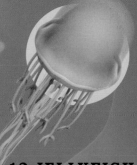

12 JELLYFISH

MIDNIGHT ZONE
The deepest, darkest part of the ocean is called the Midnight Zone.

It is always dark here, and this zone is still unexplored, because we are just now developing technology that can withstand the extreme cold. That's what makes the creatures that live down here so extraordinary.

CAN YOU FIND?

VENTFISH

VAMPIRE SQUID

ANGLER FISH

STARFISH

SLIME EEL

SHELLINGTON'S JOURNAL

TUBE WORM

Octonauts, report back to HQ!
The Octopod is the finest vessel in the
seven seas. It's an undersea home and a
first class research vessel all-in-one. With
a powerful bubble engine, who knows
where the Octonauts will explore next!

CAN YOU FIND?

 **4 OCTOPUS**

 **6 PARROT FISH**

 **4 SNAPPING SHRIMP**

 **3 CUTTLEFISH**

 **6 SEAHORSES**

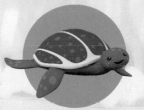 **1 LEATHERBACK SEA TURTLE**

 **7 GIANT CLAMS**

 **3 PUFFERFISH**

 **13 ANEMONES**

 **3 SEA SNAILS**

 **12 KELP FISH**

 **2 MORAY EELS**

ANSWER KEY

SUNLIGHT ZONE: TIDE POOLS

SUNLIGHT ZONE: TIDE POOLS
You may have been to a tide pool when you were a cub.

These pools of trapped seawater are formed when the tide goes out. When the tide comes back in, these pools are covered with water again. There are tough sea creatures that live here, because they have to live with constant changes in their environment.

CAN YOU FIND?

8 ANEMONES
HERMIT CRAB
SEA URCHIN
KWAZII
24 BARNACLES
6 SHELLS
9 STARFISH
5 CORAL

SUNLIGHT ZONE: KELP FOREST

SUNLIGHT ZONE: KELP FOREST
In a kelp forest, each tall kelp plant protects many creatures. At the top, fish glide beneath the leaves, and at the bottom near the roots, crabs and urchins can easily hide. It's a bit hard for a gup to get through, though!

CAN YOU FIND?

SWELL SHARK
4 SEA SNAILS
2 CUTTLEFISH
7 SEA HORSES
OCTOPUS
8 KELP FISH

SUNLIGHT ZONE: CORAL REEF

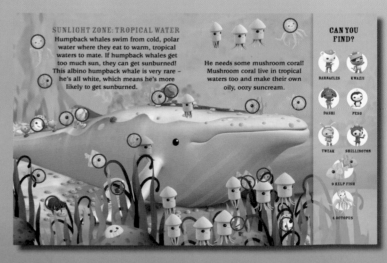

SUNLIGHT ZONE: CORAL REEF
Coral reefs are like busy underwater cities filled with lots of different types of animals. The coral are actually tiny creatures that are alive. To build a coral reef, live coral grow on top of old coral skeletons. Larger animals live in the reef too, so if anything happened to the coral, all the animals would have no place to live.

CAN YOU FIND?

MORAY EEL
GIANT CLAM
SNAPPING SHRIMP
CUTTLEFISH
OCTOPUS
PUFFERFISH
LEATHERBACK SEA TURTLE
7 SEA URCHINS
7 PARROT FISH

SUNLIGHT ZONE: JELLYFISH BLOOM

SUNLIGHT ZONE: JELLYFISH BLOOM
When jellyfish find a place they like with plenty of food, lots of jellyfish will go to that place at the same time. This is called a "jellyfish bloom". But watch out – their tentacles will sting if you touch them!

CAN YOU FIND?

12 SMILEY SEA URCHINS
4 OCTONAUTS SYMBOL
7 STARFISH

SUNLIGHT ZONE: TROPICAL WATER

SUNLIGHT ZONE: TROPICAL WATER
Humpback whales swim from cold, polar water where they eat to warm, tropical waters to mate. If humpback whales get too much sun, they can get sunburned! This albino humpback whale is very rare – he's all white, which means he's more likely to get sunburned.

He needs some mushroom coral! Mushroom coral live in tropical waters too and make their own oily, oozy suncream.

CAN YOU FIND?

BARNACLES
KWAZII
DASHI
PESO
TWEAK
SHELLINGTON
9 KELP FISH
4 OCTOPUS

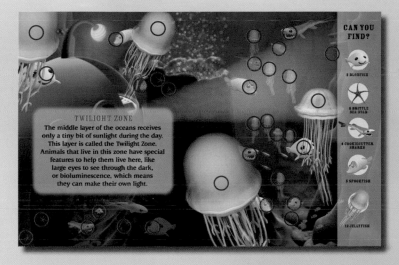

Can you go back and find:
The Octonauts?
Gup A, B and E?
Which sea creature
is your favourite out of
the ones you've spotted?

OCTONAUTS

Dive into action with these super, splashtastic Octonauts books!

 The Amazing Octopod — A Pop-Up and Play Adventure

 and the Scary Spookfish

 and the Whitetip Shark

 and the Electric Torpedo Rays

 and the Great Penguin Race

 to the Rescue! — Sticker Scene Book

 and the Decorator Crab

 and the Great Penguin Race

 and the Whale Shark

 Desert Island Doodle and Sticker Book — Draw, colour and stick with the Octonauts!

 and the Giant Squid

 and the Marine Iguanas — A Lift-the-Flap Adventure!

 and the Flying Fish

 Pirate Playtime Sticker Activity Book

 and the Monster Map — A Lift-the-Flap Adventure!

 and the Orcas

 Meet the Crew

 and the Undersea Eruption

 Go Go Gups! — GUP-C, GUP-D, GUP-E, GUP-B

 Ready for Action in the GUP – A!

 Ready to Race in the GUP – B!

 Little Library — Discover, Explore!, Rescue!, Protect!, Save the Day!

 and the Great Christmas Rescue!

 Octopod Adventure — Drive the Octopod through the ocean deep!

www.theOctonauts.com

www.simonandschuster.co.uk